Our Head Teacher is a Super-Villain

Written by Tommy Donbavand

Illustrated by Julian Mosedale

Collins

Yellow eyes

Miss Carr stood at the front of the classroom and fixed us with a strange stare.

"She's doing it again," I whispered to Holly, who was sitting beside me.

"Doing what?" she asked.

"Looking at us with her yellow, swirling eyes," I said.

Holly nodded. "All the teachers are doing that spinning eye thing now."

"Silence!" bellowed Miss Carr. "You're only allowed to speak if you want to say 'I'd like to do extra hard Maths!'

"I'd like to do extra hard Maths?" I laughed.

"Thank you for that, Max Foster!" Miss Carr announced. "You can stay after school to do extra hard Maths!"

"What?!" I cried. "No, I didn't mean that I wanted ..."

The bell rang for lunchtime and everyone jumped to their feet.

"Sit down!" shouted Miss Carr.

Everyone did as they were told.

Miss Carr held up some sheets of paper. "These are the updated school rules, written by our wonderful new head teacher, Mr Roberts," she said. "You must do exactly as they say from this moment on. I want everyone to take a copy for their parents."

We all took a list of rules to put in our bags.

"Look at this!" I hissed, reading the first line. "Rule one: No pupil will be allowed out at playtime unless they have passed a daily spelling test."

But Holly didn't reply. Instead, she grabbed my arm and we waited till everyone had left the classroom.

"We're not supposed to be in here at lunchtime," I said.

"And our teacher's eyes aren't supposed to spin round in their sockets!" said Holly. "Something's wrong."

"You're telling me something's wrong!" I exclaimed, looking at the new school rules. "Rule two: Pupils must eat cabbage stew or sprout surprise for lunch. Yuck!"

"Things have been strange ever since Mr Roberts took over as head teacher last week," said Holly.

"Strange?" I said, waving my sheet of paper in front of her. "Rule three: All PE will now take place outdoors – no matter what the weather. That's not strange – that's cruel!"

Holly scowled. "We need to find out what's going on."

"I agree," I said. "But not today ... I promised I'd play football at lunchtime."

Holly pointed to the next rule on the list.

"Rule four: All pupils are banned from playing football." I read aloud. "OK, we need to find out what's going on."

The staff room

Holly and I crept out of the classroom and made our way quietly across the school hall.

We reached the staff room door.

"Wait!" I whispered. "What if the teachers are in there?"

"Only one way to find out," Holly said.

We opened the staff room door and stepped inside.

In all my time at Riverside Primary School, I'd never been in the staff room before. I don't know quite what I was expecting – but it wasn't this ...

It was so boring!

There were just chairs, a table, some bookshelves, a cupboard and a place for the teachers to collect their mail.

"They're called pigeon holes," said Holly, noticing where I was looking. "And look – the teachers have all got a list of new school rules in there, too."

I pulled one of the sheets out and read a line.
"Rule five: Pupils are not allowed to smile."

Holly looked surprised. "That's really odd."

I shrugged. "You haven't seen me during a science test ...
I never smile!" I opened the cupboard – and froze.

"We're looking for clues," Holly said, rifling through the magazines on the table. "Anything that might give us an idea about what's going on …"

I said nothing.

"Max!" Holly snapped. "Are you listening to me?"

I nodded, staring at the six teachers tied up
and gagged in front of me in the store cupboard.

"I'm listening," I said, "and I think I may have
found a clue ..."

Super-villain!

Miss Carr – the REAL Miss Carr – was fighting against the ropes holding her arms in place, as were the other five teachers alongside her.

I reached inside the cupboard and pulled the gag from her mouth.

"Max! Holly!" she gasped. "The teachers with swirly eyes are all robot clones! You have to watch out for the new head teacher, Mr Roberts! He's a – "

" – a super-villain!" finished a voice behind us.

Holly and I spun round to find Mr Roberts standing behind us, smoothing down the wrinkles in his brown suit.

"You're a super-villain?" I scoffed, looking Mr Roberts up and down.

"Yes," said our new head teacher uncomfortably. "What's wrong with that?"

"You don't look like a super-villain for a start," I said. "Not in that brown suit!"

Mr Roberts sneered. "Then, how about this ..."

He began to spin on the spot. After a moment, there was a flash of light and Mr Roberts stopped turning. He was now dressed in a beige jumpsuit with a letter "D" on the front and a brown corduroy cape.

"I'm Doctor Dull!" he cried. "It's my mission to rid the world of excitement!"

Holly took a step forward. "All excitement?" she asked. "Like shopping for clothes?"

Doctor Dull sneered. "Especially shopping for clothes!"

"Stand back!" I said to Holly. "I can handle this ... Although, let's agree to keep clothes shopping on the banned list after we're done. That really is dull ..."

"Try your hardest, boy!" barked Doctor Dull.

Joke time

I stared Doctor Dull in the face. "OK. What do you call a man with a sea gull on his head?" I asked.

Doctor Dull frowned. "I don't know," he admitted. "What do you call a man with a sea gull on his head?"

"Cliff!" I smiled. One or two of the teachers in the cupboard chuckled.

Doctor Dull reeled back, as though injured by some powerful weapon.

"Keep going!" urged Holly. "Tell him another joke!"

"Tell me about the man with five legs …" I demanded.

"I … I can't!" said Doctor Dull, staggering backwards.

"His trousers fitted him like a glove!" I yelled. I heard sniggers behind me.

"Argh!" grunted Doctor Dull, down on his knees. "No more!"

But I wasn't ready to give up just yet. "Where do astronauts leave their spaceships?" I roared.

Doctor Dull fell to the ground. "I don't know!" he gasped.

I smiled. "At parking meteors!"

Behind me, the teachers laughed out loud.

Doctor Dull held his hands to his ears. "I can't stand the laughter!" he howled. There was a growing fizzing sound, and then Doctor Dull disappeared in an explosion of brown mist.

Holly and I raced to untie our teachers.

"We'll deal with those rotten robots!" said one of the teachers, as they ran out of the room.

"How can I ever thank you, Max?" asked the real Miss Carr.

"Well ..." I said, with a smile. "How about no homework for the rest of the school year ..."

"Nice try!" beamed Miss Carr. "Let's get out of here."

But, as we made for the door, Holly slammed it shut and turned the key in the lock. "I can't let you do that," she said.

"Why not?" I demanded.

Holly's eyes turned yellow and started to swirl. "Because letting you escape is not on the list of new school rules ..."

Max and Holly's school rules

1. Look out for teachers with yellow swirly eyes!

2. Sneak into the staff room.

3. Defeat
a super-villain.

4. Free the teachers!

5. Don't get turned
into a robot!

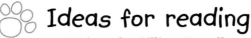

Ideas for reading

Written by Gillian Howell
Primary Literacy Consultant

Reading objectives:
- predict what might happen on the basis of what has been read so far
- discuss and clarify the meanings of words, linking new meanings to known vocabulary
- listen to, discuss and express views about a wide range of stories

Spoken language objectives:
- use spoken language to develop understanding through speculating, hypothesising, imagining and exploring ideas
- give well-structured descriptions, explanations and narratives
- select and use appropriate registers for effective communication
- maintain attention and participate actively in collaborative conversations

Curriculum links: Art; Citizenship

Interest words: villain, swirly, weird, swirling, cruel, pigeon, clones, beige, corduroy, mission, excitement, weapon, astronauts

Word count: 1,212

Resources: pens and paper, art materials

Build a context for reading

This book can be read over two or more reading sessions.

- Look at the front cover and title. Ask the children to if the head teacher looks like a super-villain.
- Ask them to say where the story is set and to speculate on what effect a super-villain might have on the school. Ask what sort of story they think this might be, based on the cover, i.e. serious or humorous.
- Turn to the back cover and read the blurb. Ask the children what they think *swirly* means and to suggest any synonyms they can think of.
- Ask the children to suggest ways in which school rules could be *weird*.

Understand and apply reading strategies

- Read p2 to the children using an expressive voice for the characters' dialogue. Point out the use of the adjectives *swirling* and *spinning* and praise the children for suggesting *spinning* as a synonym.